D1366355

THE ROYAL BRICKYARD

THE ROYAL BRICKYARD

by
DOROTHY C. HASKIN

BAKER BOOK HOUSE
Grand Rapids 6, Michigan
1959

Library of Congress Catalog Card Number: 59-15529

Printed in the United States of America

CONTENTS

1 THE ROYAL BRICKYARD

Exodus 2:11, 12)
(Hebrews 11:24, 25)

Prince Moses sprang off his chariot and stepped to the entrance of the Royal Brickyard of Pa-Ramses. He tossed to the Egyptian gatekeeper the small scroll announcing his appointment by Ramses II as "Royal Inspector of Brick-making" and strode inside the sprawling walled enclosure.

The thud of filled molds being stacked on top of one another, the harsh commands of the overseers and the scratch of stylus on stone as the scribes carefully recorded the number of stacked bricks filled the air.

Pity gripped Moses at the sight of row upon row of kneeling Hebrews filling brick-molds with mud mixed with straw. Their bony bodies were covered with only a skimpy breech cloth knotted in front. The Egyptian taskmasters in white linen skirts, carrying thick lashes, strutted up and down between the rows of workers, striking the back of any slave who paused to draw a deep breath. But the instant a taskmaster saw Prince Moses, he bowed respectfully.

Prince Moses stepped from slave to slave, checking the evenness of the bricks. They cringed before him, fearing his displeasure. He squared his shoulders and half-smiled, knowing, *They are my people. I would rather suffer affliction with them than enjoy the pleasures of the palace.*

The molded bricks were piled high and tied onto the ends of yokes. Slaves lifted the heavy yokes onto their thin shoulders and staggering, carried them down the aisles to be added to the pile after pile of bricks baking in the sun. Suppressing a desire to help the men with their loads, Prince Moses followed the line of slaves down the long aisle to where they were stacking the new bricks.

This was the first time he had been inside the brick-yard. At the palace he had heard the chiefs of tribute brag about the work done. And when the overseers reported to the chiefs of tribute, he heard enough to sense the ill-treatment that his people received. Now he had come to see for himself. If possible, he wanted to help.

A shrill scream of pain echoed through the alleys of bricks. Startled, Prince Moses looked around but the men continued with their work as if nothing unusual had happened. There was another howl of pain. *Where does it come from?* He could not see over the tall piles of bricks into the other aisles. The slaves glanced toward the sound but continued their stacking. The scream of anguish came again. Prince Moses hurried down the alley and at the end of the row of bricks, he stopped.

Lying stretched out, his face against the black earth, was a Hebrew. A taskmaster was beating him with a heavy scourge of tough, pliant Syrian wood. With each bite of the lash, the slave writhed and screamed in pain. Prince Moses recognized the Hebrew as Dathan, whom he had met when secretly visiting the home of his brother, Aaron. And he had seen Morar, the taskmaster, when he came to the palace with his reports.

"Listen!" Prince Moses ordered in a commanding tone of voice, his dark eyes flashing. "Stop beating that Hebrew!"

"What authority have you to give me orders?" Morar faced Prince Moses defiantly.

"I'm the new Royal Inspector, appointed by the Great Ramses II."

Morar caught the tip of his lash with his left hand and his eyes smoldered with anger.

Prince Moses looked down at the whimpering Dathan. "Go, tend your back."

Dathan, with blood streaked across his back, half-crawled, half-stumbled beyond the wall of bricks.

"Morar, who gave you authority to beat that Hebrew as if he were a dog?" Prince Moses said.

"By the gods Ptah, Amon and Seb, Dathan deserves a beating," Morar answered with a surly nod. "He half does his work and grumbles all the time, sneaking off here to get out of work. Why shouldn't I treat him as the slave he is? These low-bred Hebrews with their moanings and groanings deserve one hundred lashes daily."

"Why, you ——" Prince Moses' temper rose even higher at Morar's scornful attitude toward his people. He glanced quickly to see if anyone were looking and seeing no one, he raised his arm and struck Morar a sharp blow across his face. Taken off guard, Morar staggered and fell against a pile of bricks, toppling them over. He fell to the ground, a dozen of the bricks crashing on his face and shoulders.

Moses stared, waiting for Morar to move. The man groaned but lay still. *I didn't hit him that hard, but ——.* Moses knelt beside the Egyptian, pushing the bricks aside. There was a deep gash in Morar's temple and his blood flowed out, running down his face. Moses ripped off a piece of Morar's linen skirt, lifted Morar's head and tried to staunch the flow of blood. Morar gasped, shivered and then lay still. The blood seeped from the wound.

With sudden fear, Moses realized, *He is dead! I have*

killed him. Now Pharaoh will order me killed. I can't die. I have to help my people. That's why I asked to be inspector, to see how I could help them. I can't die!

Sweat trickled down Moses' forehead. He drew back, letting Morar slump to the ground and looked around frantically. Then he thought, *No one knows what I did! The bricks hid me from the others. If I bury Morar before anyone sees me, no one will ever know what happened to him!*

He pushed Morar's limp body against the bricks and feverishly began digging in the black sand. He scooped up handful after handful of black earth and tossed it aside. He measured Morar's body with his eyes, figuring the size hole needed. With frenzied strength he scooped up more and more dirt. *In my favor is this sandy soil. If only I can dig fast enough!*

He began to breathe in short gasps and decided, *The hole has to be big enough!* He turned Morar's body over and dumped it into the shallow grave, face down. With swift, desperate movements he pushed the pile of sand back over the body, completely covering it, filling the hole until the ground was even.

He stood up and stamped on the earth with his feet, pounding it until it was smooth, thinking, *What more can I do?* He hurriedly piled bricks on top of the grave until it looked like any other pile of drying bricks. *They are a little out of line because I piled them so fast. But I'm inspector and I'll never order anyone to move them. The bricks can stand here until they crumble to dust.*

He brushed the sand off his skirt and slapped his hands together, knocking off the loose dirt. He decided, *I must hurry to the palace and change my skirt.*

He gave a last nervous glance around. There was a damp spot of blood on the ground. With the toe of his sandal he worked the blood into the ground. Then he straightened his shoulders and, with a deliberate tread, he walked back between the long rows of bricks. He determined, *I'll sphinx it out. Only Dathan knows we even quarreled and surely when Morar's absence is questioned, Dathan will be too grateful to stir up suspicion.*

He reached the area where the Hebrews were pouring the mud and straw into molds. The chief overseer stepped over to Prince Moses and said, "I trust you will make a favorable report to the Great Pharaoh."

"Everything seems to be in order. I'll be back in the morning." Then glancing at his skirt, Moses muttered, "This certainly is a dirty place."

He did not wait for an answer but strode between the entrance doorposts and stepped into his gold inlaid chariot. The charioteer, Meti, flicked the horses' flanks with his whip. The high-spirited animals arched their necks and galloped along Marsh Road, the wide stretch of sandstone blocks that led across the marshes toward the Nile dike.

Prince Moses glanced at his hands and saw that they were trembling. He clenched his fists behind his back and braced himself, his over-six-feet of brawn looking every inch a prince. His sandals were pronged and of well-oiled leather. He wore a knee-length white linen skirt and a blue girdle with three jeweled tabs hanging in front. His hairy chest was bare to the hot sun. His blue and white striped headdress hung with fullness in the back, protecting his neck. His lips were full, his nose prominent and his amber eyes deep-set under thick black eyebrows.

Meti guided the horses onto the broad Nile dike. *My*

people built this dike, dug this canal, all for the glory of Pharaoh, slaving from dawn to dusk. It isn't fair! Chariots jostled Moses'. Men scurried out of the way of the horses. Women, their wares in huge baskets on their heads, walked along, calling, "Onions, leeks, garlic! Get your fresh vegetables here!"

Prince Moses realized, *These people are busy with their own affairs. Yet how quickly they would raise a cry if they knew a member of the royal household had killed a man!*

The chariot passed a woman, with a baby slung in a shawl on her back. The serious-brown-eyed baby stared at Moses and seemed to accuse, *You killed Morar!* Moses slunk to the other side of the chariot, warning himself, *I mustn't think such things! No one knows! No one knows!* But despair filled him. *I planned to do such great things and instead I have become a murderer!*

Meti turned onto the Royal Road, driving past three of the massive sandstone obelisks Ramses had erected to tell of his brave deeds. Then, reaching the tall, brick wall of the palace, he turned in the wide entrance and reared the horses to a stop. Prince Moses jumped off the rear of the chariot and walked along the pathway, between the full-leafed palm trees.

The fragrance of the myrtle filled the air. A gardener carefully weeded a bed of chrysanthemums. Bees wound their way toward the hives. Small ponds, with lotus buds floating in them, dotted the garden. An ibis, with its curved beak, fed on the bugs among the scandix with their large yellow petals.

Moses turned to the right, to the living quarters of the palace and climbed the three wide steps leading to the long courtyard that divided the men's apartments from the women's. He admired, *I've been in the palace at Thebes and at Memphis but this is the most beautiful courtyard of them all.*

The pavement was rose-colored tile. Forming a shady colonnade on both sides were tall pillars, carved with scenes from the lives of the pharaohs, Seti and Ramses. Stretched between the columns were wide awnings to keep out the hot sun. Huge potted palms gave touches of greenery.

Prince Moses walked by three young princesses seated on a carved bench, with harps in their laps, chanting a hymn to the gods. Beyond them, standing near a bowl of goldfish, was a nurse, holding a baby in her arms. His bright eyes watched the darting fish. Moses smiled at him, thinking, *Another little prince, Prince Meneptah's first-born. Though he was named for Harmhab, the first pharaoh of this dynasty, his chances of reaching the throne are few. The palace is too full of princes.*

Princess Bithiah, wearing a sheaf of pleated yellow linen, walked toward him. A warm smile crossed her pointed face as she called, "Prince Moses! The Great Ra is gracious to permit me to see you today."

"Ah, Princess-Mother, it is always a pleasure to see you, but today I am weary. Please, do excuse me."

"No, now that I have found you, I refuse to let you go." She waved her slender hand toward a chair and sat on a mat on the floor. Drawing both knees up in front of her, she clasped her arms around them and rested her face on her knees.

Moses dropped into an ebony chair, inlaid with gold. He did not want to stop to talk to anyone but he could not refuse the Princess Bithiah, who was in a sense his mother. It was she who had rescued him when his own mother, the

Hebrew Jochebed, had set him adrift in a basket on the Nile River. He respected Princess Bithiah and loved her dearly. She had married and had other sons and daughters but always she gave him the place of the oldest.

The years had dealt kindly with her. Her darkened eyebrows gave her face a quizzical expression. Her thick hair was still black and she wore it parted in the center and hanging slightly below her shoulders, with the ends curled. Her skin was clear olive and around her neck she wore a gold collar with lapis lazuli hanging from it.

"Where have you been that you are so tired? I've been looking for you."

"I've been at the Royal Brickyard." The memory of Dathan's bleeding back stirred him and he exclaimed, "Princess-Mother, this cruel treatment of my people cannot continue!"

"Why do you call them your people? You should be loyal to us, to me, who has given you a home."

"I owe much to you, Princess-Mother, but the tie of blood is strong. And I know that some day The Eternal will deliver my people."

"The Eternal, The Eternal," she repeated. "Moses, the way you talk about the gods is sacriligious, as if yours were the only one. You're little better than an atheist. It is well you do not talk to the others as you do to me, or the priests would report you to my brother as a trouble-maker."

"Listen, The Eternal is the one God."

She stretched her hand into a shaft of sunlight between the awnings, her gold bracelets catching the light of the sun. "How can you deny the Great God Ra when you can see him in the sky and feel his warmth on your body?"

"The warmth is not God. The sun is not God. God is

greater than the sun. God created it. Some day Egypt will suffer for her multiplying of gods, one for each day of the year. And the priests are the worst, deceiving the people with their charms and magic."

"If there is only one God, why doesn't he reveal himself?"

"He will. Some day He will. I know He will."

"To you?" Her brown eyes opened wide with interest.

"Not to me, but some day God will raise up a prophet from the midst of my brothers."

"I would think he would reveal himself to you. You are a true worshipper of him and you are a good man. Except a little quick-tempered." She reached out, broke off a strip of palm leaf and held it between her even white teeth.

Moses dropped his eyes. *I am not a good man.* He noticed the black sand beneath his square fingertips and again he was filled with fear. *I must clean my nails. By now Morar must be missed and the search begun for him or his murderer!*

"Temper in a man is like the rising of the Nile. It is terrible at the time but it enriches the soil, and so temper shows that a man has spirit. I like a man with temper, but ——." She threw away the strip of palm with a gesture of hopelessness. "You have strange ambitions."

"To help a slave people is not ambition. I've seen enough ambition here at the palace to fill a pyramid. Besides, now, I never expect to help them."

"Why?"

The sound of loud, angry voices reached him. Relieved that he could avoid his mother's question, Prince Moses stood up and looked toward the end of the courtyard. Servants and princes were gathered in an excited group.

Princess Bithiah stood beside him. "Let us see what is happening!"

2 THE PALACE AT PA-RAMSES
(Exodus 2:13-15)

Princess Bithiah broke into a light run. Prince Moses' long steps kept pace with her. They reached the crowd from where the angry voices had come. The servants stepped aside respectfully, allowing the royal couple to move into the center of the group.

Prince Meneptah and Prince Meri-Atum faced each other. Their dark-skinned bodies, clad in blue skirts and yellow girdles, were taut with anger. Their faces were flushed a purplish-tan. Prince Meri-Atum pouted, "But you promised that if I gave you the oil you would give me a scarab. Now you have used the oil, I want my scarab."

"I won't give you a thing!" Prince Meneptah tossed his head arrogantly and his voice was loud and harsh. "I don't care if the oil did come from Syria, it wasn't as fragrant as you said it was. So I won't give you the scarab."

"But you gave your word!" Prince Meri-Atum insisted.

"Meneptah would promise an obelisk with a fence around it if he wanted something," Princess Bithiah whispered to Moses.

"He wouldn't even keep his word to The Eternal," Moses answered.

"I will go to father and tell him that you are a cheat." Meri-Atum's high-pitched voice grew shrill.

"By the life of Pharaoh, you do and I'll ——." Prince Meneptah raised his arm to strike his brother. Prince Moses sprang behind Meneptah, caught his arms and pinned them to his side. Prince Meneptah struggled to free himself but Moses held him fast.

"Thank you, Prince Moses. My brother isn't himself today, or is he?" Prince Meri-Atum slurred and sauntered down the courtyard, followed by his friends and servants. One carried a huge plumed fan, another a tray with a gold inlaid cup and violet-glazed jar of water on it, and a third, two cushions.

Moses relaxed his hold. Prince Meneptah swung around, facing Moses. His thin nostrils quivered. "I'll see to it that you regret interfering in my affairs."

Moses did not answer but looked at him with disgust. The constant bickering by the princes, the coveting of each other's possessions was distasteful to Moses.

Prince Meneptah stalked away, followed by his friends and servants.

"He will hate you for this," Princess Bithiah whispered. "I must persuade him that you helped him by keeping him from striking Meri-Atum." Princess Bithiah started after Meneptah.

Moses stared at the stately woman following her nephew and realized, *I did do him a favor but he thinks I publicly humiliated him. Perhaps Princess-Mother can reason with him, but I doubt it. If it were Meri-Atum who was in the wrong, he would be more inclined to listen to her. But Meneptah is head-strong. Fortunately for Egypt he is fourteenth in line to the throne, so that he has slight chance of ever being pharaoh. But I'd better beware of him. If he ever learns of what happened at the brickyard, he will use it to avenge himself.*

Prince Moses walked across the courtyard to the wide entrance that led to the men's apartments. He took off his sandals and, carrying them by the straps, continued along the long, cool hall to his room.

Once behind the closed door, he did not call his servant but poured water over his feet into a copper basin, washing them. Then he poured water over one hand and the other, washing them. He dried his hands and feet on a rough linen towel. From the table he took a slender ivory pick and dug the tell-tale black sand from under his fingernails.

Clean, he ripped off his soiled skirt and, putting on another, he flung himself on the divan, settling his head on the wooden headrest. Twilight shadows crept through the window grating, and in the sooty darkness his thoughts tumbled like the water paddles at the crest of the Nile.

Has my quick temper brought me to a dungeon, or perhaps the lash, or even the sharp knife? It is a bitter end, but I have never been happy, never fit into this place.

Always he had been an aloof little boy. The fact that he enjoyed studying, listening to the teachers, poring over scrolls and clay tablets, set him apart from the other princes. They were ever seeking a magic charm to quicken their minds so they could avoid studying.

And, too, in his heart were strange memories. Sometimes the look of a woman on the street in front of the palace stirred him. Or his deep feeling about God. But it was only after his fight with Prince Meneptah that his Princess-Mother told him who he really was.

After that his pity for his kin separated him from his palace associates. How could he laugh with those who made slaves of his people! Even when Seti went to the realm of the dead and the Hebrew boy babies were no longer killed at birth, the lot of Moses' people was bitter with toil.

One consuming desire burnt within Moses' heart. He would deliver his people, some day, somehow! To this end he devoted all his energy. He studied hard, absorbing all the culture and knowledge of the Egyptians. And whenever possible, he sneaked to the home of his natural family, asking questions, absorbing the tradition and culture of the Hebrews.

His dedication to his task made him shun the Egyptian princesses. Marriage with one of them would only hinder him. He allowed himself the relaxation of the companionship of children and his Princess-Mother. He told her of his acute ache to help his oppressed people. She warned, "Moses, your interest in these people will only bring you trouble. Why throw your life away? They are but slaves and you, by every ray of the great Ra, are destined to become a great man."

A great man! Moses lay on his couch in his room in the palace, remembering what she had said, knowing, *I've ruined my chances. All my years of study! All my dreams! Perhaps I was as arrogant as one of the priests to expect The Eternal to use me to deliver my people. But now, dare I hope that He will even be merciful to one who has taken life? How I dread returning to the brickyard tomorrow!*

But return, he must, if he were to behave like an innocent man! The next morning Prince Moses had Meti drive him to the brickyard. There, he jumped lightly off the rear of the chariot, ordered, "Wait for me," and strode through the entrance.

He forced himself to walk leisurely to the area where the bricks were being made. A Hebrew laid a molded brick on a pile and paused, looking wearily at the sky. An overseer struck him across the bony shoulders with his lash. The man flinched in pain and bent over his work. Wincing at the sight, Moses walked on. *I must see if the grave is still covered.*

He walked between the high walls of bricks to where the men were patiently piling the freshly molded bricks, and beyond, to the end of the last row. There, two men were scuffling, raising the dust. He stopped in surprise. *Can it be that an Egyptian is fighting with a Hebrew? No, both wear only loin cloths. They must be Hebrews. Why, one of them is Dathan!*

Moses sprang toward the men and pushed them apart, holding them firmly by their shoulders. "Listen, why are you fighting your own kin?"

"Who made you a judge over us?" Dathan sneered. "Do you think you can kill me as you killed the Egyptian yesterday?"

Startled, Moses glanced from one man to the other. Both faces accused him. He dropped his grip on their shoulders, and without another word, fled between the piles of bricks. But one thought filled him, *I've got to get to the palace and find a way to keep word of the murder from Pharaoh's ears!*

He ran through the entrance, sprang onto his chariot and ordered, "Drive like a hawk to the palace."

Meti stared at Moses, a question in his dark eyes.

"The palace, and quick!" Moses repeated, asking himself, *Does he merely wonder why I'm going back so soon, or does he know the truth? How many has Dathan told? How could I expect loyalty in one bred like a slave?*

Meti slapped the reins on the flanks of the sorrel horses and the high-spirited beasts broke into a gallop. They passed scores of Hebrews working in the marshes, gathering straw for the brick-making, and each one seemed like an enemy. *Soon everyone will know I have killed a man! The word will travel like fire across a field of stubble.*

Meti made a sharp turn onto the dike and a woman darted out of the way of the horses.

"Don't ——" Moses began, then checked himself. He had been going to say, "Don't kill anyone else."

Meti drove like fury along the dike, dodging in and out of the other chariots. Suddenly, among those coming toward them, Moses saw a chariot whose gold leaf trim dazzled brightly in the sun. He realized, *It is someone from the palace. Perhaps after me!* He was cold with fear until he recognized the blue and white sunshade of Princess Bithiah's chariot.

She waved at him and her charioteer reined his horses to a stop.

"Hold it!" Moses ordered. Meti pulled the reins, stopping the horses. Moses jumped down, strode to the Princess' chariot and stared at the woman who had given him a mother's love. Her black hair was caught off her face with gold clips. Around her slender neck was a collar of gold chains and her reed-like figure was clad in a russet gown, with a girdle of gold fastened in front by a turquoise studded ornament. *How disappointed she will be in me!*

He lifted her to the ground and they walked to the edge of the dike. For a moment Moses watched the Nile flow smoothly to the sea and the men ply by in their papyrus skiffs. Then, fearful of her answer, he asked, "What is wrong?"

"This morning after you left, word spread through the palace that someone had told my brother you murdered one of the overseers at the brickyard. You didn't, did you?"

"Princess-Mother, The Eternal knows that I did!"

"I remembered how upset you were yesterday and though my heart said this rumor could not be true, I was afraid that it was. I had your servant get me your cloak and set out to warn you." She passed a long, white wool mantle to Moses. "You know my brother's reverence for life. If you return to the palace, he will order you killed. You must hide."

"Should I run away like a coward? No, rather I will go, not because of Pharaoh's anger but because I believe The Eternal would have me live."

"Always you talk of The Eternal! Yet you admit that you must hide to save your life. If he is so great why won't he protect you at the palace?"

"Because while The Eternal is almighty, He is also just. I have done wrong and must pay for my sin."

"What good is a god who is just? I don't want that kind of a god. I want one who will do as I tell him when I need help."

"The Eternal is also merciful. This is not the end. But I am not ready to go on a journey. I need my cup, another pair of sandals ——."

"But you dare not go to the palace for them!" She reached into the pouch hanging from her girdle and drew out a handful of gold rings and bracelets. "Take these. I brought them for you."

"Thank you, Princess-Mother. You are ever thoughtful of my need! May The Eternal allow me to help you someday." He put the jewels in the pocket of his belt. "I will catch the first caravan going East, perhaps to Ascalon or Gaza. When Ramses goes to the realm of the dead I will return. Already he has been on the throne twenty-seven years. He can't live forever."

"He might live to reign sixty years."

"Thirty-three more years? Impossible! Please order Meti to return to the palace. I go but I will return."

He looked at her affectionately, then slung his mantle over his shoulder and mingled with the throng on the dike. He knew he looked like an Egyptian. He was a little taller, more broad-shouldered but, until Pharaoh sent out an alarm, no one would look at him with suspicion.

He made his way toward the meeting place of the caravans, with each step taking him from the ease of the palace into the unknown.

3 A WELL IN MIDIAN
(Exodus 2:15-20)

Moses could hear the brays of the donkeys as he approached the loading place of the caravans; then he smelled the mixture of sweat and spices. The mart was on the fringe of the city, beside the Nile. Sweaty Hebrews unloaded the bales and baskets from docked boats. Shrewd merchants from Aram, Moab, Edom and the East bickered and bargained. Huge square warehouses lined three sides of the huge mart and in the center were tethered donkeys and camels.

Moses stood, staring, wondering, *Where shall I go?*

Ben-Anath, a Syrian caravan leader, spotted Moses and came up to him, asking, "You want passage to Elath? to Midian?" He rubbed his hands against each other. "I have the best passage. High on a camel. You see everything."

"Midian?" Moses hesitated. In his many journeys through the countries over which Pharaoh ruled he had not been to Midian. It sounded as if it might be a lonely place. *Perhaps it is best.* He reached into his pouch and pulled out one of his Princess-Mother's gold rings.

Ben-Anath's brown eyes shone with greed. He moistened his lips. "Two rings and I give you your food, too. Melons, dried fish, plenty of corn."

"When do you leave?" Moses felt in his pouch for another ring.

"Soon. Already we are loaded." Ben-Anath stretched

forth his hand. Moses dropped the two rings into it. "Come this way."

Ben-Anath, with oily courtesy, showed Moses the back of a camel he could share with a load of corn. Moses took his place. The stiff-necked camel swayed and rose. Then Moses waited and watched. Two other caravans lined up and trotted out of the square but still Ben-Anath fussed with his loading. Moses grew more and more uneasy, watching each stranger who entered the busy mart. *Is he looking for me?*

At last, toward late afternoon, Ben-Anath lined up his ten camels and led them out of the mart, out of the city, through the suburbs. They travelled all that night. At times Moses dozed fitfully; at other times he watched the stars and prayed to The Eternal for forgiveness and safety.

By morning the caravan reached Succoth. There, Ben-Anath stopped to water his camels and to rest. Moses climbed off the camel, relieved to stretch his cramped legs and to talk to Ben-Anath and his helpers.

After the mid-day heat had passed, the caravan continued on its journey. They went to Ethan, the temple of the sun god, crossed between the Bitter Lakes and the Red Sea, then turned southeast, going along the eastern shore of the Red Sea. Sometimes the days were clear and hot. Other times the caravan travelled through such wind-raised clouds of dust that Moses could scarcely see the camel ahead of him.

At the scattered inns, oases and towns, Ben-Anath stopped, selling his corn. Moses watched him, as with a combination of bragging and shrewdness, he drove his bargains. After Ben-Anath completed his business he would chatter of the people along his route to Moses. He listened to every detail of the lives of the nomadic people, *I must learn their ways if I hope to hide myself among them.*

The moon had thinned to a narrow crescent by the time the caravan reached the tip of the Sinai peninsula and turned northeast toward the land of Midian. One late afternoon, Ben-Anath told Moses, "This is Midian. It is not much of a place, but no doubt if you wait here, someone will come along and help you find the rest of your way."

Moses nodded. He had chosen his place by chance and was ever fearful of letting Ben-Anath know he had no real reason to come to Midian.

The caravan headed north, toward Elath. He watched the cloud of dust made by it grow smaller and smaller, feeling utterly alone.

He dropped onto the edge of the large, round stone well, with a thin cover of slate over its mouth. The earth around the well was muddy and showed the footprints of sheep. He grew hopeful, *When the shepherds come to water their sheep, I'll talk to them. Maybe they will let me stay with them. My people have been shepherds since the days of Abraham. It is fitting that I should become one. It will be a relief to lead a quiet life for a while but not too long! I'm too active to do nothing long.* He rose and walked impatiently around the well, the thick mud caking his sandals.

The sun had begun to sink behind the mountains when he heard the approaching bleating of sheep. He tossed the end of his mantle over his shoulder and wanting to see who was coming stood partly hidden by the feathery flowers of a tall acacia tree. The cloud of dust turned into a herd of plodding sheep and with them, in their varied colored robes and veils were — Moses counted, *one, two, three, four, five, six, seven girls!* They were all ages, the smallest about ten, the oldest fleshy with years, and one of them quite pretty, with quick, darting hands.

One of the older girls let down the bucket into the well, pulling it up and passing it to another girl to empty into the stone trough. The sheep crowded up to the trough, guzzling the water.

"Away with you! Away! Away!" came a loud command.

Moses looked around, recognizing the words as being spoken in Hebrew and thankful that he spoke several languages. Two shepherds stalked by him toward the well. Moses hoped, *Perhaps these men can help me!* Both men wore dark robes, long sheepskin abas, striped abajas on their heads and carried staffs. Behind them jogged a large herd of sheep.

When the men reached the girls, the older man raised his staff threateningly and demanded, "You and your sheep get out of here. There is not enough water for both herds and we need the water for our sheep."

"We need water for our sheep, too," the older girl answered in a quiet manner. "It may be there is enough for both herds, for we have only begun to draw water."

An old sheep raised his head and cried, "Baa, baa." Down the line the sheep chorused, "Baa, baa," and began crowding toward the girls' herd. They bleated at one another, pushing and jostling.

"I warn you, get away!" the shepherd shouted.

The smallest girl whimpered in fright. The prettiest girl drew her close, throwing her veil over the young one's face.

Moses' spirit flared, *Is there no justice in the land? Has not The Eternal created enough for all?* He strode toward the shepherds and in their language said, "The girls were here first and they are going to water their sheep if I have to fight both of you."

The shepherd glanced at Moses' short, white skirt, at his striped headdress, and snarled, "Who gave you authority, O Egyptian, in the land of Midian?"

"My strong right arm gives me authority." Moses clenched his fists and muscles flexed in his bronzed arms.

"We don't want to fight with a stranger. We'll wait," the shepherd excused. Then with loud curses, he and the other shepherd drove their herd away from the well.

With a feeling of contempt for the man because he would not fight, Moses turned to the oldest girl. "Let me help you."

"If you will," she accepted gratefully.

Moses dropped the bucket into the water, filled it and lifted it. Time after time he poured water into the trough, letting it splash onto the ground and his feet. With much bleating the sheep drank their fill.

The oldest girl thanked Moses for helping them and then, with her staff, urged the sheep away from the trough. The prettiest girl smiled shyly at Moses, drew her green veil over her face and began helping her sisters herd the sheep toward home.

Moses walked away from the well and stood under the acacia tree. The shepherds glanced at him with hatred in their dark eyes and began drawing water for their sheep. Moses knew, *No use asking them if I can spend the night in their tents! They wouldn't do anything for me now. Yet I have to fight for the weak.*

Disheartened, he watched the shepherds drive their sheep down the dusty road. Then he sat on the wall, resting his head in his hands. The shadows slipped down the purple mountains. He remembered the dining hall at the palace, with servants carrying in trays piled high with melons, fish and pastries. That was his home and he had forfeited his right to it. *Life is like a bowl. It takes skill and time to mold it, fire it with glaze and yet, in one second, one can drop it and smash it to pieces.*

"Egyptian," came a low voice.

Startled, he looked up. He had not heard footsteps in the soft mud but the prettiest of the girls, with the youngest, had returned. In hurried sentences, she explained, "Jethro, my father, sent Keturah and me for you. We told him the way you helped us and he said you must come and break bread with us."

"Thanks be to The Eternal!" Moses answered, as he stood up.

"Come with us."

Moses walked down the road between the pretty girl and her sturdy sister, in her short tunic. She looked at Moses with frank curiosity.

"My father's name is Reuel," the older girl chattered. "Jethro is his honorary title, as priest of Midian. He is ruler of the Midianites, and also of the Cushites who have settled in this district. My name is Zipporah and this is my sister, Keturah. She was named for our ancester Abraham's second wife."

Moses nodded. *How pleasant it is to be among my own people!* "Your father has no son?"

"We have a brother, Hobab, but he is away in Sinai, looking for a new grazing place for the sheep. You are an Egyptian and have had no experience with sheep, have you?"

"It is true that the Egyptians are not shepherds," he evaded her question, sensing, *She thinks I am an Egyptian because of my dress. If I do any explaining, it will be to her father.*

They reached a thick grove of waist-high reeds, planted as a wind-break. They circled them to a row of tents made with side walls of bricks and roof of heavy brown cloth held up in front with branches from trees. Behind them were the sheep corrals and one of the daughters in a purple robe tended the sheep. The air was filled with a chorus of baas.

A tall, well-built man with a full, brownish-gray beard, wearing a brown robe and a brown and yellow striped abaja, strode toward Moses. "Welcome to our tents, O Egyptian! The Eternal be gracious to you for all you have done for my daughters this day! Will you break bread with us and share a mat for the night?"

Moses bowed his head in reverence. "The Eternal has been kind to bring me to your tents! I am both hungry and weary."

The men chatted of Moses' trip from Egypt until the girls served them bowls of steaming lamb and herbs. After they had eaten, Jethro invited Moses out of the rising night wind into his tent. The flap was dropped. Jethro sat on a mat, surrounded by his daughters. On the right sat Zipporah and Keturah and on the left, Zeruiah, Rachel, Leah, Milcah and Tirzah, like a cluster of inviting grapes. Moses squatted uncomfortably on a mat opposite his host, longing for one of the palace chairs.

"Is it true that Pithom and Pa-Ramses are cities of great beauty?" Jethro asked.

"The cities are filled with many large buildings but

they are also forts. Ramses realizes he must guard against revolt from within and attack from without."

"Tell me, is Ramses as great a man as we hear that he is?"

"He will go down in history as one of the greatest, if not the greatest pharaoh in Egypt."

"As a warrior and a builder?" continued Jethro.

"Both. He has able overseers of the army to fight his battles and he travels all over Egypt, inspecting the great temples and other important buildings. On those he likes, he has the name of the pharaoh who built them chipped off and his own name chiseled in its place. When Ramses is dead, the record of granite will proclaim that he was great."

"I heard rumors that that was what he did, but I am surprised that you, an Egyptian, would admit that Ramses is not the great man he would have us believe."

Moses studied the friendly faces of the girls and their father and decided, *I will admit my kinship to them.* "I am not an Egyptian. I am a Hebrew. You, as a descendant of Abraham, must remember that his great-grandson, Joseph, was sold into Egypt."

"It was my ancestors who headed the caravan to which Joseph's brothers sold him. They took the boy into Egypt and sold him to Potiphar."

"And a wicked woman plotted for him to be put in prison," Zipporah spoke up. "But he interpreted Pharaoh's dreams about the famine and became a great man. Father has told us."

"And during the famine, Jacob took his sons and grandsons into Egypt," the young Keturah added.

"Yes," Moses nodded. "When the Hebrews first came

to Egypt they were well treated, given the land of Goshen in the delta for their homes. The Egyptians welcomed them because they were craftsmen, builders and farmers, while their people were shepherds. However, when the Hyksos were driven from the throne and a pharaoh who knew not Joseph reigned, the Egyptians began to treat my people as slaves."

"Well do I know it!" said Jethro.

Moses glanced questioningly at Jethro and his daughters. *If only I could settle down here until Ramses dies! He can't live forever. The seed of death is in all of us from the minute we are born, due to our heritage from Adam. How much of the truth dare I tell Jethro?*

4 THE TENT OF JETHRO

(Exodus 1:8-22, 2:1-10
Hebrews 11:23-26)

Moses tried to read Jethro's face in the light of the flickering wick in the bowl of oil. *He seems kind.* "You and I must be about the same age. Surely you have heard of the cruel decree of Seti, when he was pharaoh?"

"I know." Jethro's dark eyes burned with anger.

"What decree?" Zipporah asked, and the other girls stared at Moses with curiosity on their faces.

"Seti had trouble with the Syrians. He would conquer them but they wouldn't stay conquered. Fighting them occupied much of his time and attention. Fearful that he would have trouble at home when at battle, he ordered the midwives to kill the newborn Hebrew boy-babies when they took them to the troughs on the Nile to wash them. There was great sorrow among the Hebrews. My parents, Amram and Jochebed, had two children, a six-year-old girl, Miriam, and a three-year-old boy, Aaron. When Jochebed knew she was to bear another child, she and Amram spent long hours talking about how, if it were a boy, they might save his life. They cried unto The Eternal for help.

"Since she was afraid it might be a boy, Jochebed did not call the midwife. Amram cared for her when her baby was born. With despair and delight, they saw that I was a boy. To them it was a goodly child whose life must be spared. They hid me, stifling each little cry, but by the time

I was three months old, my crying became so loud they knew I soon would be discovered.

"Jochebed went to the Nile, cut thick stalks of papyrus, wove a basket and daubed it with mud from the river. When it dried, it was waterproof. She put me in this cradle and went to a place on the Nile where Pharaoh's daughter was accustomed to bathe, fenced off from the crocodiles. Mother placed my little boat among the bulrushes, where it would not drift. Telling Miriam to watch what happened, she went back to her hut to pray."

Zipporah, a soft light in her dark brown eyes, interrupted, "Her mother heart told her how to protect her son!"

"Or The Eternal!" Jethro reverently reminded.

Moses nodded. How wonderful it was to be with those who believed in the one God! How weary he had grown of the talk of Ra, Osiris, Ptah and the others! He went on, "As Mother hoped, Princess Bithiah, the fourteen-year-old daughter of Seti, came with her maid-servants to bathe. Bithiah noticed the little ark nestled among the bulrushes and ordered, 'Get me that strange object.'

"One of her servants waded into the river until she was able to reach the basket and brought it to the young princess. I howled loudly. Princess Bithiah said, 'This is one of the Hebrew children whom my Father ordered killed, but I will save him. One can't make a difference and he is so alive and healthy.'

"My sister, Miriam, was a brave girl. She stepped from behind the palm tree and asked, 'Shall I go and call one of the Hebrew women to nurse the little boy for you?'

" 'It would be well! Do so,' the Princess ordered.

"Excited, Miriam went to Mother and told her what had happened. Mother went to where the Princess Bithiah was holding me in her arms. She gave me to Mother, and agreed to pay her for nursing me. This was the blessing of The Eternal, because if anyone questioned Mother's having a boy baby, she could say that the Pharaoh's daughter had told her to care for me. Mother nursed me, trained me and taught me of The Eternal."

"How long did you stay with your mother?" asked Zipporah.

"When I was not quite four, she gave me up for the second time. It must have broken her heart almost as much as it did the first time, for she knew she would never see me again. She dressed me in my best white robe and took me to the palace.

"Princess Bithiah was delighted to have me with her. She was a warm-hearted woman and her father did not object to her whim to have a son. She adopted me and kept me in her apartment until I was six. Then she became the wife of one of Seti's favorite advisors and I was given a room in the men's apartment of the palace. I was taught with the other princes and considered myself one of them. There was even talk that someday I might be pharaoh. Seti favored Bithiah and her son might well have ascended the throne.

"Then Seti died. There was much wailing and a pompous funeral. Bithiah's brother, Ramses II, ascended the throne. Shortly afterwards, I was playing in the courtyard with Meneptah, one of Ramses' sons, a few years younger than I. I bragged, 'When I am older, I shall be pharaoh.'

"Meneptah's face grew red with anger and he said, 'I shall be pharaoh. Not you! You can never be pharaoh. You're one of those stinking Hebrews, not Princess Bithiah's real son.'

"With one swing of my fist, I knocked him down. How dare he say I was not Bithiah's son! She was my mother! Even though he was younger than I, I jumped on him, pounding him. Two servants dragged me off and took me, shaking, to Princess Bithiah. They told her I had been fighting my cousin and I defended, 'But he said you were not my real mother!'

" 'The rumors have finally reached you,' she said. She told the servants to leave and drew me beside her on the couch. Her eyes grew damp with tears as she said, 'It is not my wish to tell you this but there is no keeping a secret in this palace. I love you as my own son but you are really one of the Hebrew children. When you were three months old I saved you from the Nile. That is why I named you Moses, *Son of the Nile.*'

"I was shocked but after that I refused to be called the son of Pharaoh's daughter. I became interested in the Hebrew people and learned all I could of them. I lost all desire to be the pharaoh. What value were the treasures of Egypt when my own people were suffering? No longer did I join in the pleasures of the palace which last but for a season. With Princess Bithiah's permission, I went to visit my mother and father.

"I had my own chariot and often went to their hut, to listen to Mother tell the stories of Adam and Eve, of the tower of Babel, of the journey of Abraham, and the stories of Isaac, Jacob and Joseph."

Moses paused and studied Jethro's face. *Has The Eternal brought me to a friend with whom I can share my secret longings?* He said, "I have grown up with the conviction that these facts should be written down for our people, that they should know our story in a pure form."

"It is true that they should. Perhaps you will be the one to write a history of the Israelites. You are well-educated."

"I can use papyri and stylus but our history must be written by a man of God and I am not. My mother hoped I would be. I was with her when she was dying. She told me, 'Moses, The Eternal did not save your life in vain. You are destined by God to deliver your people from slavery.'

"I answered, 'Truly, Mother, I believe The Eternal had a purpose in sparing my life, and I shall so live that I may be worthy to be the deliverer of Israel.'

"There was a great sadness in my heart as I saw her spirit leave to join her fathers. Again I knew grief when, about two years later, my father died. But I continued seeing Miriam, even after Hur took her to wife,* and Aaron, after he took Elisheba to wife. I rejoiced with Aaron when he welcomed into his home little Nadab and Abihu."

"Did not those at the palace object?" Jethro asked.

"Yes, I suffered the reproach of their scorn, and though I knew my friendship with the Hebrews ruined my chances for advancement at the palace, my heart was with my people."

"Did you ever take a wife?" Zipporah asked. Interest on the faces of all the girls quickened.

"No, I did not. I couldn't marry a Hebrew girl and I would not marry an Egyptian. I wanted to be free when the time came for The Eternal to use me."

"Apparently The Eternal did not use you. Why?" Jethro asked.

"I had gone along, feeling that The Eternal was preparing me. I had learned to read and write in both Egyptian

---

***The Bible does not tell us that Miriam became the wife of Hur, but Josephus says so.**

and Hebrew. I studied their codes of law. I studied everything I felt a leader should know. The time came when I felt I was ready for a closer relationship with my people. I went to Pharaoh and asked for the position of inspector of the brickyards. Overseeing an oppressed people is a thankless job and so he willingly appointed me. It was in the early afternoon that I rode to the brickyards ——."

Each girl leaned forward, as if sensing that Moses had reached the important point in his story. Jethro urged, "Go on."

"I killed a man!"

"Oh!" A groan broke from the throats of several of the girls. The two younger girls moved closer together, as if that gave them a feeling of protection. Keturah put her hand over her mouth and her eyes opened wide. Zipporah edged slightly toward Moses, pity on her face.

"It is a great sin to take life but sometimes there is a reason. Tell me how it happened."

Moses bowed his head in his hands and once more he saw the limp body of Morar as he lay in his shallow grave. Moses lifted his drawn face and told them, "Morar was beating one of the Hebrews and I couldn't stand it. I sent Dathan away and in anger knocked Morar down. He fell against a pile of bricks, taking them with him. One of the bricks hit him on the temple, cutting a deep gash. The blood flowed. He gasped for breath a few times, then died. Thinking no one had seen me, I buried him, but apparently Dathan had been watching from behind the bricks. The next day, rumors went through the palace. Dathan must have talked. I knew Pharaoh would order me executed and so I ran away. I have come this far by caravan and now I must find a place to live in exile."

In the measured tones of one used to handing down a sentence, Jethro said, "Moses, there is mercy with The Eternal. He knows that sin is a part of us. Some day He will reveal a fit sacrifice for sin. Until He does, I can only forgive those whose sins are different from my own. I cannot say which sins are worse. You are welcome to live with us and help Hobab and the girls tend the sheep."

"You are most generous."

"And now, girls, to your mats. All too soon the sun will shine on bush and stone."

Slowly the girls rose. Keturah suppressed a yawn. Zipporah gave Moses a friendly smile, drew her green veil over her face and went behind the curtain at the end of the room. The other girls followed her.

"Let us step out for a breath of air," Jethro invited.

The two men stepped outside the tent. Moses glanced up at the stars. How near they seemed! So much nearer than in Pa-Ramses! And there were so many! No wonder Abraham had been filled with awe when The Eternal had said that his descendants would be numbered as the stars in the heaven.

Jethro folded his arms across his breast and with hesitancy in his voice, said, "You spent most of your years at the palace. Surely there are many of their practices of which you approve."

"Many. They are exceptionally clean people. Their laws are fair."

"But they practice plural marriage. Do you favor it?"

"Listen, to live with plural marriage is to see how evil it is! Such fighting and scheming among the sons of Ramses for the most honor! Such scheming among the wives for a favored position! The peace of a house is cursed by multiplying wives."

"Here it is when two women grind at the mill that the gossip starts."

"Besides, I have noticed that when a man has many wives, there is always one he loves above the others. Ramses loved Nefretiri more than any of his other wives but she died when still young. She was the mother of Meri-Atum, and that is why I expect him to be the next pharaoh. Perhaps the depth of love that can exist only between one man and one woman proves best that it is the plan of The Eternal for a man to have but one wife."

"Abraham had one wife at a time. Isaac had but one wife. I think Jacob would have been content with Rachel, and happier."

Moses could hear the murmur of girls' voices in the tent behind him. *Perhaps Jethro will give me one of his daughters for a wife if I stay here. Zipporah would be a pleasant companion; and while I wait for The Eternal to reveal what I am to do next, I must build a life.* He clenched his fists. *Surely, I won't have to wait long!*

5 THE BACKSIDE OF THE DESERT
(Exodus 2:21–3:6)

Moses and Zipporah stood by the wall of reeds in front of Jethro's tent. Moses stared at Keturah, a short distance from them. She was kneeling on the ground, a stone trough before her, in which she was kneading dough.

"How long have I been with you?" Moses tried to figure.

"Ten times the hills have been bare and cold. Ten times they have worn a new robe of green," Zipporah answered.

"In those years Keturah has grown into a young woman. The next thing we know one of the shepherds will come along and take her away from us. When I came, she was a pudgy child!"

"You've changed, too," Zipporah reminded with a twinkling laugh. "We thought you were an Egyptian but no one would think so these days. Your old linen skirt made a fine rag to polish my copper kettles. Anyway, I like you better wearing a full beard and in a brown robe."

"You girls were kind to make it for me," he patted his robe and turned his attention to Zipporah. She was attractive in her mustard green robe, held in place by a wide leather girdle. Her dark hair peeked from beneath her yellow veil and her eyes were bright. He had grown to enjoy her companionship above that of her sisters.

"It is not fitting for Keturah to be married until after Milcah, Tirzah and I are married. I know that Zeruiah,

Rachel and Leah are happy in their own tents, but ——."
She carefully eyed the ground and said, "It would be proper for me to marry next."

He put his arm about her shoulder and drew her toward him, to where she fitted snugly into the curve of his arm. She looked at him, surprised by his sudden show of affection. He said, "These years have been made rich by your kindness. You have been the one who looked after my wants, who told me the news, who was content to sit silently beside me when I was in a quiet mood."

"I wanted to," she answered simply, her eyes shining with love.

He put his left hand into his pouch, drew out six small turquoise stones and he held them in the palm of his hand. "These are among the few things that I have left from Egypt. Would you like to have them, perhaps in a bracelet?"

"How lovely!" She freed herself from his arm, took the turquoise in her hands and studied them. "I think I would like a bracelet, as you suggested." She handed them back to Moses and continued, "But why are you giving me such a valuable gift?"

"Zipporah, dear, do try to understand me. As long as your older sisters were at home, it was not proper for you to marry."

"But now it is."

"Yes, and it is only fair to you that I should make up my mind. Listen! My heart yearns for you but I hesitate to take a wife because I hope that Ramses will die and I can be free to return to Egypt, to help my people."

"Moses, you have seen me refuse the attention of other shepherds because for me there could be no one but you, even though I know you aren't like other men. There is a *

To middle Of Next Page

bodies. Ben-Anath was seated on the edge of the well, eating dates. He waved at Moses, "How goes it, friend?"

"All is well," Moses answered and dropped onto the edge of the stone well beside his friend. He listened patiently while Ben-Anath told the details of his journey from Egypt.

"But I know," exclaimed Ben-Anath, "it is news of the palace that you're waiting for."

"How is the great Ramses?"

"Well and strong as ever! That man is destined for a long life. Another of his sons has gone to the house of the dead ahead of him."

"Who?"

"Meri-Atum."

"That cannot be! I had hoped that he would be the next pharaoh."

"He will never be pharaoh now."

distance in your spirit. But men who serve The Eternal need a wife to care for them, and ——." Her voice grew husky. "Should I have even that small part, I would consider myself blessed of The Eternal!"

"It is not good for man to live alone, nor do I want to." He put his arm around her shoulder and patted her gently. "Zipporah, be patient with me. Today Ben-Anath is due to pass through with his caravan. I want to talk to him."

She nodded, but her eyes were misty.

Resolutely, he started down the road toward the well. He had kept up his friendship with Ben-Anath by meeting the caravan leader whenever he passed through Midian.

When Moses reached the well, the caravan was already there. The camels were on the ground, resting. The drivers were lying beside them, their heads against the beasts'

"And the Princess Bithiah?"

"She yet lives. I tell you, they are a long-lived people, these Egyptians."

Moses nodded and listened while Ben-Anath talked the hot hours away. When the day began to cool, Ben-Anath, whip in hand, lashed the camels and their drivers to their feet and the caravan started northward.

Moses watched until the dust became a blue on the horizon. *I shall hope no longer.* With decision-squared shoulders, he walked to the tents of Jethro. Zipporah was standing near the high windbreak of reeds. Moses went to her, took her hands in his and studied her face. Already the sun and wind had brought tiny lines at the corners of her eyes. The relentless years were snatching her youth away. *The desert life is a hard one, but it need not be a lonely one.*

"Zipporah, hope dies slowly within me. But Ben-Anath says my enemies still live. After ten years, I shall wait no longer. Let us ask your father if he will consent to my taking you for my wife."

"Moses, I will become your wife, but I know your ambition has not died. Your heart is as much set toward your helping your people as ever, like the pushing of a root toward a spring of water."

"I cannot kill what is in my heart though it seems hopeless." He folded her closely in his arms. "Meanwhile, The Eternal is gracious to grant me the comfort of love."

Later Moses thanked The Eternal again for the comfort of love when he held his first-born son in his arms. He stood in front of his tent with his father-in-law, Jethro, looking at the tiny red mite in his arms. "Listen, I shall call him Gershom!"

"Meaning *a stranger in a strange land.*"

"True! I was a stranger at the palace during my youth. Now, I am a stranger in a strange land. Unless The Eternal permits me to lead my people into a land of their own, I always will be a stranger."

"You never forget!" Jethro said in a tone of amazement.

"I have paid for my sin by exile, but I never forget my suffering people." He thought of the nights when he had paced the desert under the stars, praying to The Eternal, seeking a way to help his people. Always when he knew Ben-Anath was due, he had hoped, and always Ben-Anath brought word that Ramses II lived on.

The days went on. He watched his son grow. He celebrated when Milcah and Tirzah went to the tents of their husbands. He felt a kinship for Keturah when she refused to marry, choosing instead to care for her father. The tents of Jethro grew smaller with the years.

Rejoicing came again when he sat in his tent by Zipporah's side. She lay on her mat, her face drawn and weary. Moses held his second son in his arms and, looking at the sleeping mite, decided, "Listen, I shall call him Eliezer!"

"You mean, *God is my helper?*"

"Yes. For truly The Eternal has been my helper here in Midian."

"I, too, have helped you," she defended with spirit.

He looked kindly at the woman who had done a hundred things for his comfort, cooked his food, rolled up his mat each morning, lit the wick each evening. "I appreciate you, dear. It is only that I long to be used by The Eternal."

How impossible it seemed that The Eternal would ever use him! Years passed. His sons grew to manhood. His flocks increased. The seasons followed each other as continuously as the Hebrew slaves had filled the brick molds in Pa-Ramses. Ben-Anath died and there was no longer news of Egypt — only a spirit of waiting, a feeling of frustration.

The day came when Moses stood outside Jethro's sheepfold, realizing that it had been nearly forty years since he had left Egypt. He was still straight and vigorous. The passing years showed only in his gray-streaked hair and the tempering of his spirit.

Zipporah came out of their tent. The years had made her more full of figure and lined her face. And her mouth had become one thin line, as if it had been drawn with one swipe of the stylus. Life with a restless man had made her defensive. She handed Moses a cloth wrapped around some dates and rolls. "Here is your lunch."

He put the lunch in his pouch, hanging from his girdle, beside his gourd of water. "I am going to pasture the sheep near Mount Sinai."

"That means you will be gone overnight. You men always want to go far." Her voice had the shrill tone of a high-pitched flute.

"The sheep need a change of pasture." He threw back the wooden bars of the sheepfold. "Atoti, Atoti," Moses called. He had named the lead sheep for the man who had been leader of Pharaoh's chariots. The name seemed to keep alive his hope that some day he might lead men instead of sheep.

Atoti slapped his broad tail and started away from the corral, the other sheep following him. Moses made his way among the sheep to Atoti's side. They trotted along the road a short distance, then started across the wilderness toward the mountains. The sun was pleasantly warm on his back. As he walked he mused, *Dear Zipporah, she is a good wife! She keeps the tent clean but she thinks I should be satisfied to herd these sheep year after year. When she senses that I'm unhappy, she considers it her fault. It isn't her fault. It's only that I feel I'm wasting my life as a sheepherder.*

Something pulled at him. He stopped and loosened his aba which was caught on a thorny bush. Then he plodded slowly on, the sheep trotting in front, beside and behind him, raising whirls of dust. At each step, he stuck his staff deeply into the earth, to keep his balance on the rocky ground.

The sun rose higher and higher. At noon Moses crouched in the shade of an acacia tree and ate a few dates. The sheep chopped the stray green leaves off each bush, stopping now and then to baa.

Odd, how a woman's talking amuses a man until he is shut up in a tent with her! Then it becomes like a constant baa, baa of the sheep . . . noise without meaning. Yet The Eternal allowed me to be tented with Zipporah's chatter that I might learn to control my temper. Only He knows if I will ever win that battle!

A bug crawled onto Moses' hand. He knocked it off, rose and began walking. *How I have learned this stretch of land during these forty years! I think I know every stream, spring and wady in Sinai.*

When the sun dropped behind the purple mountains, he gathered the sheep close around him, ate more dates and stretched out in his warm aba. For a few minutes he studied the stars, noting their patterns, then he fell into a deep sleep.

In the morning he led the sheep to a spring. While they watered, he washed and then ate a roll. Then he started back the way he had come the day before, hoping to reach his tent by night.

As he walked along he noticed a yellowish-red glow. *What is that? It looks like a fire!* He quickened his step, going nearer the blaze of light. *A fire would be dangerous in this dry desert!* As he neared the flame, he paused, marvelling, *Odd, there is no sound of crackling as there usually is when something burns!* He stared at the fire. *What wonder is this? Though the flames burn brightly, the bush does not burn. I will go close and see why this thorny bush does not burn.*

"MOSES, MOSES," a VOICE called out of the flaming bush.

Moses stopped still. *Who can be calling me out of that burning bush? It must be The Eternal!* With awe filling his heart, he whispered, "Here am I."

"DO NOT COME NEARER," came the VOICE again, clear in the desert stillness. "TAKE OFF YOUR SANDALS, FOR THE PLACE WHERE YOU ARE STANDING IS SACRED GROUND."

Moses stooped down and with trembling hands, unloosened the laces of his sandals. He kicked them off and then, with great wonder, went and stood in front of the burning bush.

"I AM THE GOD OF YOUR FATHERS, THE GOD OF ABRAHAM, THE GOD OF ISAAC, AND THE GOD OF JACOB."

It is The Eternal! Moses flung his arm in front of his face. *I dare not look upon The Eternal. I, who have long sought God, now I hear Him, am afraid!*

6 THE FOOT OF MOUNT SINAI
(Exodus 3:7–4:19)

"I HAVE SEEN THE TROUBLES OF MY PEOPLE WHO ARE IN EGYPT AND I HAVE HEARD THEIR CRY, CAUSED BY THE OVERSEERS. I KNOW THEIR SORROWS," the VOICE in the flame continued.

They have suffered long, O Eternal! Moses thought, but he was too frightened to speak.

"I WILL DELIVER THEM OUT OF THE LAND OF EGYPT AND BRING THEM INTO A GOOD LAND FLOWING WITH MILK AND HONEY, INTO THE LAND OF THE CANAANITES."

Surely The Eternal is promising my people the finest land in all this region! It is the fulfillment of His promise to Abraham!

"THEREFORE WILL I SEND YOU TO PHARAOH, THAT YOU MAY BRING THE ISRAELITES OUT OF EGYPT."

"Who am I, that I should go to Pharaoh to bring the Hebrews out of that country?"

"CERTAINLY I WILL BE WITH YOU! THIS SHALL BE A SIGN THAT I HAVE SENT YOU. WHEN YOU HAVE BROUGHT THE PEOPLE OUT OF EGYPT, YOU SHALL SERVE ME UPON THIS MOUNTAIN."

Slowly Moses raised his eyes and glanced at the barren place. *How wonderful it would be to serve God even in a place like this! Yet, if I go to Egypt and tell the Hebrews that The Eternal has sent me to deliver them, they will mock me.* His awe of The Eternal and his fear of people struggled within him, until the fear of people was stronger and he dared ask, "What will happen when I go to my people and say to them that the God of their fathers has sent me to them? And they will ask me, what is His name? What will I answer?"

"I AM THAT I AM. THIS IS MY NAME AND THIS IS MY MEMORIAL UNTO ALL GENERATIONS. GO, GATHER THE ELDERS OF ISRAEL TOGETHER AND SAY TO THEM, 'JEHOVAH, THE GOD OF YOUR FATHERS, THE GOD OF ABRAHAM, OF ISAAC AND OF JACOB, HAS APPEARED TO ME SAYING, "I HAVE SEEN THAT WHICH IS DONE TO YOU IN EGYPT, AND I HAVE SAID, I WILL BRING YOU OUT OF THE TROUBLES OF EGYPT INTO A LAND FLOWING WITH MILK AND HONEY." ' "

Long have I wanted to help my people, but now The Eternal tells me to do so, I know I am not able. Pharaoh will never let his laborers go. He is dependent upon them to build monuments in his honor.

"THE PEOPLE WILL LISTEN TO YOUR VOICE AND YOU AND THE ELDERS SHALL GO TO PHARAOH AND SAY TO HIM, 'JEHOVAH, OUR GOD, HAS MET WITH US AND NOW LET US GO THREE DAYS' JOURNEY INTO THE WILDERNESS THAT WE MAY SACRIFICE TO OUR GOD.' I KNOW THAT PHARAOH WILL NOT LET YOU GO BUT I WILL STRETCH FORTH MY HAND AND STRIKE EGYPT WITH MY WONDERS AND

AFTER THAT, PHARAOH WILL LET YOU GO."

Surely I must believe you, O LORD! He formed the different name for The Eternal slowly. *It is a long time since the days of Abraham when he called Eternal Jehovah, THE LORD, but that is the name by which He would reveal Himself to the people. It is a name closer to their hearts than The Eternal. I do believe the LORD could deliver us but even if Pharaoh did let us go, we would have nothing with which to build a home in the new land.*

"AND I WILL GIVE MY PEOPLE FAVOR IN THE SIGHT OF THE EGYPTIANS AND MY PEOPLE WILL NOT GO OUT EMPTY-HANDED."

The LORD can read every thought in my mind! Moses realized with alarm.

"EVERY WOMAN SHALL ASK OF HER NEIGHBOR JEWELS OF SILVER AND OF GOLD, AND CLOTHES, AND YOU SHALL PUT THEM ON YOUR SONS AND YOUR DAUGHTERS AND YOU SHALL TAKE TOLL OF THE EGYPTIANS."

It would be only fair payment for their many years of labor! But I am not capable of being their leader. He protested, "But they will not believe me or listen to me for they will say that the LORD has not appeared unto me."

"WHAT IS THAT IN YOUR HAND?"

Moses stared at the staff in his hand. "My rod."

"THROW IT ON THE GROUND."

Moses threw the wooden staff on the ground. It twisted into a coil, raising its head, stuck out its tiny fangs and hissed. *It is a cobra! The royal sign of Egypt!* Frightened, Moses shrank from the snake.

"STRETCH OUT YOUR HAND AND PICK THE SNAKE UP BY THE TAIL, THAT THOSE WHO

SEE YOU MAY BELIEVE THAT JEHOVAH, THE GOD OF THEIR FATHERS, APPEARED UNTO YOU."

Carefully Moses edged toward the writhing snake. *The LORD said, "By the tail." If only I could pick it up by the neck so it would be unable to bite! But ——.* He stretched out his hand and touched its slick tail. As he lifted it, the snake straightened and became his staff. Moses sighed with relief.

"PUT NOW YOUR HAND INTO YOUR BOSOM."

I dare not disobey the LORD. Moses shoved his left hand into the front of his robe. When he took it out, he swallowed a sudden lump in his throat. His hand was white with leprosy! *O LORD, don't touch my body with leprosy!*

"PUT YOUR HAND INTO YOUR BOSOM AGAIN."

Loathing to touch his chest with his hand, he forced himself to put it into the front of his robe. When he took it out, the skin was tanned and natural appearing. A feeling of relief swept through him.

"IT SHALL COME TO PASS THAT IF THE PEOPLE WILL NOT BELIEVE THE FIRST SIGN, THEY WILL BELIEVE THE LATTER SIGN, AND IF THEY WILL NOT BELIEVE EVEN THESE TWO SIGNS, YOU SHALL CHANGE THE WATER OF THE NILE INTO BLOOD."

Wonder upon wonders! Surely with all these signs both Pharaoh and the Hebrews will believe I am God-appointed! But I would be ill at ease in the palace. In the last forty years I have talked only to my family and few friends and seldom have spoken in Egyptian. "O LORD, I am not a man of words, neither in the past or even now since You have spoken to me. I am slow of speech and slow of tongue."

"WHO MADE MAN'S MOUTH? OR WHO MAKES A MAN DUMB, OR DEAF, OR SEEING OR BLIND? IS IT NOT I, THE LORD?"

It is God Who makes men able to speak but can He give me fluency of speech?

"NOW THEREFORE GO AND I WILL BE WITH YOUR MOUTH AND TEACH YOU WHAT YOU SHALL SAY."

But I know my own short-comings! If the LORD only would send someone else then I would stop complaining about living on this desert. "O LORD, I pray You, send by the hand of him whom You would send."

The flame in the bush flared higher as if in rebuke and the VOICE continued, "IS THERE NOT AARON, YOUR BROTHER, THE LEVITE? I KNOW THAT HE CAN SPEAK WITH EASE."

Moses recalled his days in Egypt when Aaron had been a leader of the Hebrews, often speaking in their mass meetings. *Aaron can speak fluently but how could I get in touch with him? I wonder if he still lives with his family in that hut on the edge of the marsh?*

"BEHOLD HE IS COMING TO MEET YOU AND WHEN HE SEES YOU HE WILL REJOICE IN HIS HEART. HE SHALL BE YOUR SPOKESMAN TO THE PEOPLE. HE SHALL BE TO YOU A MOUTH AND YOU SHALL BE TO HIM AS GOD AND YOU SHALL TAKE IN YOUR HAND THIS ROD WHEREWITH YOU SHALL DO THE SIGNS."

The flame died away. Moses stared at the thorny bush. It looked as stunted and scratchy as ever. He glanced toward the sheep, ambling along, munching on green leaves. *How queer! Did I see a vision?* He looked at his feet. He was barefooted. A bug crawled over his toe. He knocked it off and crushed it. *The vision was real!*

He walked to where he had left his sandals, sat on the stony ground and slowly, thoughtfully, laced them on. A feeling of unreality filled him. *Has the LORD spoken to me?* He picked up his staff and stared at it. It was still the plain branch of an almond tree that he had whittled into a rod. Had it been a snake a few minutes ago and God had promised it would be again? Atoti trotted toward him. He scratched the sheep's head, then said, "Come, we must go home."

He stood up, straightened his broad shoulders and started toward the tents of his father-in-law. As he walked along, he wondered how he could tell his family that God had spoken to him! It was difficult to explain.

It was so difficult that he said nothing to Zipporah, Jethro or anyone until after the evening meal. Then Moses and the others gathered on mats in front of Jethro's tent. Behind them, the sheep safely in the fold gave an occasional baa. The warm breeze brought the far-off hoot of an owl or the howl of a dog. The blue glazed sky shone with jasper bright stars.

Moses knew, *It is going to hurt to leave them.* He glanced at Jethro, grown lean and gray with the years. *I have enjoyed his friendship.* He looked toward Keturah, in her purple robe, sitting sleepily by her father's side. *Life has passed her by, by not allowing her the comfort of a husband.* Beside her sat her brother, Hobab, with a contented smile on his face. *He feels satisfied because somewhere today he has driven a shrewd bargain.* Next sat

Jedida eyeing her husband, Hobab, as if he were pharaoh. By Moses' side were Zipporah, and his sons, sitting tall and straight in their loose tan-colored robes.

Jethro's alert brown eyes searched Moses' face. "You are as full of news as a woman returning to her father's tent on a visit. What troubles you?"

"It has been many years since I left my people. I feel that the time has come for me to return to Egypt, to see if Aaron and Elisheba, Miriam and Hur and their children, are still alive." *I cannot tell them of my vision.*

"But Egypt is so far away!" Zipporah exclaimed.

Gershom nodded in agreement, but Eliezer spoke up, "If it is not too far for father to come, it is not too far for him to go."

Jethro crossed his arms across his breast and, with an official air, said, "It is right that you should visit your family. Hobab, you can take care of his sheep while he is away, can't you?"

Hobab greedily rubbed one palm against the other. "It can probably be arranged."

"You have so much to do already," Jedida purred.

"The boys can watch them," Zipporah reminded.

"I want you and my sons to come with me," Moses told her.

Gershom looked from his father to his mother with surprise, but Eliezer asked, with interest, "Is Egypt much different from Midian?"

"Much! Much! I'll enjoy showing you the sights. I wonder how many obelisks Ramses has had my people build by now."

"You won't want to stay long, will you?" Zipporah asked apprehensively.

"I don't know," Moses admitted.

"Then perhaps I ought to stay here. I've everything fixed the way I like it, and you know I can't sleep on a strange mat."

"But Zipporah, there will be times when I need you and the boys, your comfort, and ——."

Jethro gave his daughter a stern look. "You will go with your husband."

She said nothing further, but bit her lip.

"Well, I don't know ——," Gershom began.

"We'll enjoy seeing things," Eliezer interrupted him.

"We will leave in the morning," Moses told them.

The family talked a long time about Moses' proposed trip and the wonders of Egypt. Slowly, one by one, they slipped away to their tents. Moses and Jethro remained alone in the moonlight. *I wish I could tell Jethro about my plans but it is best to see what Pharaoh does.*

"I have known that you would go some day, but I thought you would wait until you knew Ramses was dead."

"I've had no news of Egypt since Ben-Anath died. Perhaps Ramses has forgotten the death of Morar. I have to take that chance."

"It is in the hands of the Lord."

He went to his tent. He could hear Zipporah's even breathing, and from beyond the curtain came the snoring of Gershom and Eliezer. Even surrounded by his family, he felt lonely. He faced such a gigantic undertaking!

"GO, RETURN TO EGYPT," came the VOICE he had heard on the desert — only now it was low, as if it were in his own heart. "FOR THOSE WHO WOULD HAVE TAKEN YOUR LIFE ARE DEAD."

A feeling of relief filled him. *So, Pharaoh was dead, at last!* He stretched out on his mat. In the morning he would begin the long journey back to Egypt and his people!

7 THE ROAD BACK TO EGYPT
(Exodus 4:20-28)

Early in the morning the tents of Jethro were awake. Zipporah rolled the things she felt her family would need on the trip into two bundles and slung them over the back of the donkey. Keturah gave her some freshly baked rolls wrapped in a cloth. Jedida brought a bowl of fig preserves.

Meanwhile, Moses put the few valuable rings and jewels he had left into his pouch. Then he turned the sheep over to Hobab's care. When everything was settled, he helped Zipporah mount the donkey. Keturah, Hobab and Jedida said "good-bye" as sadly as if the travellers were going beyond the rim of the world.

Jethro lifted him arms to heaven, and his wide sleeves fell back as he blessed, "Go in peace!"

Moses struck the donkey on the rump and with his sons walking beside him, started toward the wilderness of Sinai. He waved back at the group, which grew smaller and smaller. Sadness overcame him for he had many warm memories of the forty years in Midian.

The day was hot and wearying as the family made their way over the hilly paths. Twice they stopped at springs that the donkey might drink while they ate dates and rolls. But most of the day they plodded on.

Occasionally either Gershom or Eliezer rode while their mother walked. When they went beyond where the boys had herded sheep, Gershom stared at the strange country with passive curiosity while Eliezer eagerly pointed out the different plants. Zipporah paid scant attention to the new sights but fussed at the donkey.

Moses walked along with a quiet spirit. Again he heard the VOICE say, "WHEN YOU GO BACK TO EGYPT SEE THAT YOU DO BEFORE PHARAOH ALL THE WONDERS WHICH I HAVE PUT INTO YOUR HAND. BUT I WILL HARDEN HIS HEART AND HE WILL NOT LET THE PEOPLE GO. THEN YOU SHALL SAY TO PHARAOH, 'THUS SAYS JEHOVAH, ISRAEL IS MY SON, MY FIRST-BORN. LET MY SON GO THAT HE MAY SERVE ME. AND IF YOU WILL NOT, I WILL KILL YOUR FIRST-BORN.' "

I must prepare my sons for all that I am to do. He called them to him and began, "My people are the first-born of The Eternal. Of all the nations on earth, we were the first to believe in only one God. The other nations had a god for each village, or worshipped the sun, moon and stars."

"But God would only be one, wouldn't He?" Gershom answered placidly.

"Didn't you once say the Egyptians had a god for each day of the year? And that they treated your people like slaves?" Eliezer spoke with spirit.

"Listen, the day of reckoning is coming! They should realize that it would. They have laws telling them to be fair to others, yet they have been cruel to my people."

The afternoon sun blazed brightly. Zipporah complained, "Where are we to spend the night? On this rocky ground? Though I suppose I could sleep on anything, I'm so tired. I'm not used to riding hour after hour."

"I know, Zipporah," Moses tried to console her. "I think we'll have a comfortable place for the night. There's an inn further up the road and if we keep going for another hour —."

"Another hour! My bones will shatter like an old pitcher."

"An hour is not long when you realize that there will be a spring, a cluster of tents and a place to spread our mats."

"Not long to you, a strong man, but long to a woman away from home." She set her mouth into a grim line.

She is a good wife, he reminded himself. *She doesn't understand and how can I expect her to when I have not explained everything to her. I must tell her tonight. Perhaps after the boys are asleep. If only Aaron would come to meet me, as the Lord promised! It would be a confirmation of His word to me!*

The family rode into the long mountain shadows. The chirping of the birds grew less frequent. At last, in the distance, Moses saw a blur. Gradually it shaped into a grove of palm trees and tents beside a well.

The evening was cool by the time they reached the inn kept by Ashor, the Amalek. Ashor, followed by two gangling boys and a toddling girl, came out of a large tent, and with many bows greeted the travellers.

Groaning, Zipporah dismounted. Ashor showed Moses a tent where his family might spread their mats. Moses parted with one of his few remaining gold rings. His sons carried the mats into the tent, and then Zipporah spied the stone oven set near the well. In a few minutes, with a contented smile, she was cooking food in her favorite copper kettle.

Ashor showed Moses where, behind a wind-break of reeds, he could tether the donkey. He gave Moses hay for the animal, and then, alone, Moses knelt beside the donkey to thank The Eternal for the safe journey of the day.

As Moses waited for his meal, he saw a cloud of dust approaching. "Another traveller is coming." He watched while the dust shaped into a donkey and a person. Noticing the familiar set of the shoulders, the way the man held his head, he waited eagerly until the man brought the animal to a stop and dismounted. "Aaron, my brother!"

The brothers threw their arms about each other and kissed each other on the cheek. Moses stepped back and stared at Aaron. He was over six feet and his tanned face had a florid cast. His beard was still full and brown but his hair, though thick, was streaked with gray. Moses warmed at the sight of his brother, who had once told him the troubles of their people. "You haven't changed a bit."

"Your face is softer. You've lost the haughtiness of the palace."

"Forty years on the backside of a desert teaches a man many things. Come, meet my wife and sons." Moses led Aaron to the oven and, with his arm around his brother's shoulders, introduced, "This is Zipporah, my wife."

She smiled, nodding, and her heavy gold earrings jangled.

"This is my brother, Aaron, come from Egypt to meet us."

"You didn't tell me he was coming." Zipporah's tone was an accusation.

"I didn't know where I would meet him," Moses excused.

"The Eternal told me to come into the wilderness to meet you, but didn't tell me exactly where," Aaron explained.

"And these are my sons." Moses was proud of the manly young men in their tan robes and green abajas. "Gershom, my oldest, is like his mother. And this is Eliezer."

"How odd! My third son, born after you left, I named Eleazar. Cousins with almost the same name."

"A likeness of mind."

"Will you join us for a meal?" Zipporah invited.

Moses smiled at Zipporah, pleased that despite the inconveniences of a new place, she was hospitable to his brother.

Zipporah lifted the lid off the kettle. The smell of the steaming food filled the air. Moses sniffed it hungrily, then nodded to Aaron, "I have much to tell you, but first, tell me about your family."

Aaron squatted on the ground with Moses beside him. Eliezer and Gershom moved nearer them.

"Eleazar and Ithamar were both born after you left. All the boys are married but the two oldest have no children, so they live with us. Eleazar and Ithamar have families and live on each side of us. The houses are small and crowded."

"Conditions are not better than they were. I was afraid of that. How is Miriam?"

"She has always enjoyed good health. Her delight these days is her grandson."

"Come, let us eat," Zipporah invited and she served the men steaming bowls of gruel.

After they finished eating, Zipporah rinsed the bowls. Then she and her sons went wearily to their mats.

Moses and Aaron moved closer to the still warm oven. Moses began, "The Lord has called me to return to Egypt to lead my people out of Egypt."

"Sometime ago, when Ramses died, I thought the time might be ripe for your return."

"How old was Ramses when he died?" Moses tried to figure the age of the monarch.

"Over ninety. He outlived his thirteen oldest sons, reigning sixty-seven years. Probably the longest reign of any pharaoh."

Moses remembered that Princess Bithiah had once said her brother might reign sixty years and he had thought it impossible. But he had reigned even longer! He asked, "And my Princess-Mother, does she still live?"

"I hear that she does."

"The Eternal is merciful. I shall see her again. And who is pharaoh now?"

"Meneptah."

"Meneptah!" Moses remembered the arrogant young man whom he had known at the palace. "He will not be kind to my people."

"True, he is a hard man with whom to deal. He is interested only in power. He cares only for those of his own family. Moses, have you considered the tremendous task it will be to lead our people out of Egypt?"

"I have dreamed of nothing else most of my life."

"But consider, there are at least 600,000 men, besides the women and children. Pharaoh will never let them go. It is too large a supply of labor. And at least one-third of the Egyptians are in the army. That would be a mighty army to fight."

"Our people will go free. Listen ——." He told Aaron of the VOICE in the flame Who had told him that the time had come to deliver the Israelites and that Aaron was to be his mouthpiece. "And the LORD gave me a sign to prove to the people that He is with me."

Moses rose and picked up his staff from where it was lying on the ground. "Look." He threw the wooden rod on the earth in front of him. It began to twist and turn like a snake.

"What a marvel!" Aaron exclaimed.

"Moses, what are you doing? What is that?" demanded Zipporah as, hearing Aaron's excitement, she came out of the tent.

Moses bent down and picking the snake up by the tail, it became a rod. "It is nothing to alarm you."

"Have you told her?" Aaron asked.

"No, but I must. Zipporah, Aaron and I have been talking about my real reason for going back to Egypt. I want to see my family as I said but, too, I know that it is time for the Lord to deliver my people from slavery."

"Moses says the LORD is with him and I believe him," Aaron assured her.

Upset, Zipporah looked from one man to the other. "Pharaoh might not believe in our God at all. And if he doesn't, wouldn't it take a long time to convince him?"

"It may take a month. Perhaps two months."

"That's a long time to be away from home."

Moses studied her tired face. "I wanted the comfort of having you with me. I wanted my sons to see Egypt, but I know that the trip and the strangeness is hard on you."

"Where would we stay?"

"At my home," Aaron invited.

"At another woman's oven? I'm used to my own things. The meal was not ready as soon as usual tonight."

Moses clasped his hands behind his back and straightened his shoulders. "Now that Aaron has joined me perhaps it would be best if your returned to your father's tent in the morning. Aaron and I can join a caravan and go on to Egypt."

"And the boys?"

"Let them return with you and take care of the sheep."

"We'll have to give Hobab a sheep for taking care of them this short time. He'll expect it."

"Yes, Zipporah, we must be fair."

"Then Gershom, Eliezer and I will return home in the morning," Zipporah said, a contented expression on her face. She put her work-worn hand on Moses' arm and added, "I hope you won't be gone long."

"I will come and get you and my sons as soon as I can," he promised.

8 THE MEETING PLACE OF THE ELDERS
(Exodus 4:29-31)

In the morning Moses had stood at the edge of the oasis and watched Zipporah and his sons start back to the tents of Jethro. Later in the day, Aaron and he joined a passing caravan and returned slowly to the city of Pa Ramses in the delta of Egypt.

Moses had been pleased to see again the boat-crowded Nile, the waving palm trees, the angular buildings and towering obelisks. Too, he had been surprised at some of the changes in the city. The old loading place of the caravans had been built up with new houses and the caravans met farther out of the city. Aaron explained, "The people complained that the camels and donkeys raised too much dust."

Moses was delighted to see Elisheba again and to meet Aaron's family. Elisheba set aside a small room off the courtyard for him. And Aaron's four sons: Nadab, Abihu, Eleazar and Ithamar, asked him hundreds of questions about Sinai and Midian.

Miriam and Hur came to see him. Miriam scolded, "You shouldn't have run away when you got into trouble but come to me. I'd have found a place to hide you as we did when you were a baby."

As much as he enjoyed being with his family, in his heart there had been the continual need of facing the Israelites with his mission. Aaron sent word of the coming meeting to the brickyards and half-constructed forts and granaries, and it was whispered from man to man. After the elders had eaten their evening meal, they were to gather outside of Aaron's house.

And so, Moses, staff in hand, waited in front of Aaron's house. It was where Marsh Road, from the City of Pa-Ramses, met Ur Street, the beginning of the Hebrews' houses, and a convenient place to gather.

Besides Moses stood Aaron, Elisheba, Hur, Miriam and Aaron's four sons. The oldest, Nadab, was holding a torch. He whispered, "I don't know how many will come tonight. They spend the feast days talking of revolution, but when it comes to action, they're more sheep than goats. But I'm for a change."

"I realize that the men must be tired after working all day," Moses excused.

"Being a leader, you get out of work," Nadab chuckled as if he understood a private secret of Moses.

Moses' tanned face flushed a deep red at his inference.

A man with grayish-white hair and unevenly trimmed beard stepped out of the doorway across the street. Aaron brought him to Moses and introduced, "This is Jemuel, of the house of Simeon."

"Welcome to Egypt, though I can't see why you've come," said Jemuel.

Another man walked toward them. Aaron introduced, "This is Nahshon, Elisheba's brother."

Moses studied the tall man with the pleasant expression on his face and liked him. More and more men began to gather and Aaron introduced:

"This is Nun, of the tribe of Ephraim."

"This is Korah, of the tribe of Levi."

"This is Hanoch, of the tribe of Rueben."

"This is Palti, of the tribe of Benjamin."

The introductions continued until Moses stopped trying to remember the names. There were too many of them. The men had changed from the breech cloths they wore at work into short robes. Some of the robes were brown or blue. Others were red, yellow or green striped. Most of the men had thick heads of hair and full beards. A few were clean-shaven and wore their beards narrow like the Egyptians.

When the last introductions had been made, Aaron stepped onto a large, overturned water jar. He faced the throng of seventy or more men, with a few women standing among them, crowding Ur Street, stretching onto broad Marsh Road. "I am speaking for my brother, Moses, who has returned from the land of Midian. He has come to us because the God of Abraham, Isaac and Jacob, has revealed to him that the time for our deliverance has come."

"It is time," cried the crowd.

"We have suffered enough," said others.

"Moses and I will go to the Pharaoh and ask him to let us go three days into the wilderness to worship The Eternal."

"Pharaoh will never let us go."

"We want more than three days to worship."

"We want freedom," exclaimed the men.

"Nor do we know this Moses," came a gruff voice.

Moses' eyes searched the faces, alert ones, dull ones, trying to decide who had said that, but he couldn't.

"You may not know Moses, but he knows The Eternal."

"You say he knows The Eternal," retorted an angry voice, "but does Pharaoh know that he does?"

"God has given him a sign for Pharaoh and for you.

Wait." Aaron jumped off the water jar, "Moses, give me your rod."

"Yes, let us see what The Eternal has done especially for you," said Miriam.

Moses passed his rod to Aaron and his heart became a prayer.

"Spread out! Stand back!" Aaron ordered. "Hold the torches high!"

Nadab stepped closer to Aaron, holding a flaming torch high. The men edged forward, expectancy on their faces. "Let me see, let me see," cried excited ones. Some climbed on jars and the young ones climbed onto the nearby roof tops.

Aaron laid the staff on the overturned water jar, and it became a snake, sliding down the side of the jar, onto the earth.

"Look out!" exclaimed Jemuel, jumping back.

"It is a snake. It is!" shouted Miriam.

"He turned a rod into a snake!" ran the cry through the crowd.

"I can't see it," came an insistent voice from the rear.

Aaron picked up the tail of the snake and it stiffened into a staff in his hand.

Some of the elders crowded close to him. Others gathered in small groups, agreeing, "The Eternal has spoken to Moses. The Eternal is ready to deliver us!"

"Shall we pray?" called Aaron.

"Yes. Yes." The men bowed their heads. Aaron led them in a prayer of thanksgiving. Then he announced, "Tomorrow, my brother and I will seek an audience with Pharaoh."

"Good. That is fine," exclaimed Hur, Nahshon and several of the elders. They stood around talking to Moses and Aaron, asking questions, until Nadab's torch burnt low. Then, in twos and threes, they started back to their huts.

At last the brothers were alone in the murky darkness.

"This is a night of great promise!" Aaron said. "The greatest since the Hyksos, who favored our people, were driven from the throne. The people have accepted you as their God-appointed leader."

Moses looked from the faint lights in the crowded huts toward the distant palace of the harsh Pharaoh, and up to star-filled sky with a thankful heart. "The years of waiting are over. Our hour of deliverance has come!"

You will want to read about Israel's deliverance in the next book — *The Courtyard of Hur*.